The CHOCOLATE Thief

KATH KIRKLAND
Illustrated by Jamie Doodle

Copyright

Dedication

I dedicate this book to my late mother, Angela Tilbrook, who was a children's author. Her inspiration and dedication to write has given me the creativeness and desire to follow in her footsteps and write stories for children myself.

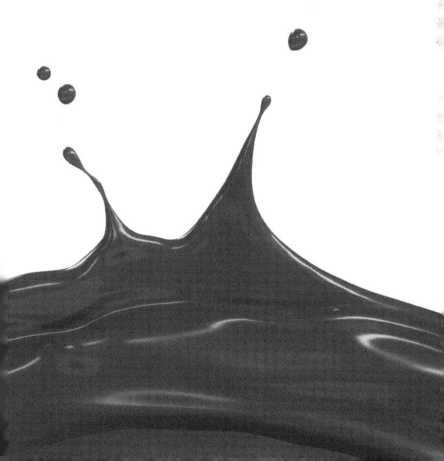

Introduction

Thank you for choosing The Chocolate Thief. I have had lots of fun writing this book for readers such as you.

I have always enjoyed reading and, now, I also enjoy writing. I grew up reading books such as those by Roald Dahl, Mary Norton and Enid Blyton. Reading lots of books has helped me understand the English language and given me the ability to write.

When I was at school, my mother was a children's author. I would return home from school every day to the sound of her electric typewriter, clicking away, loudly. I am very old and computers didn't exist then! My mother would ask me to read all of her stories she had written and then ask me if I enjoyed them? I was very privileged to be able to do this and this has now given me the desire to write and share my stories with my own son.

Kath Kirkland

Chapter one

Billy Jenkins

Friday 13th

Billy Jenkins liked chocolate. No, sorry, let me start again. Billy loved chocolate. He loved chocolate so much more than anything else. He loved chocolate more than football and he really liked football.

He loved chocolate more than his PlayStation and he really loved playing games on his console. It was obvious to other people that he loved chocolate as he had spots on his face, spots on his arms and smears of chocolate all over his clothes. Billy's friends called him Tubby, because all the chocolate he had eaten had made his tummy large, so very large.

"Nan, would you like some chocolate?" Billy asked whilst shovelling three chocolate caramels into his mouth at once.

"No, thank you. You know I really don't like chocolate." Nan turned her nose up.

"Nan, you do not know what you are missing," Billy said, whilst putting two more chocolate caramels into his mouth, and

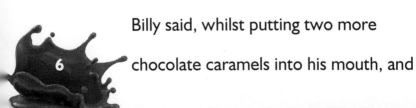

6

melted chocolate dribbled down his chin. "How can you not like chocolate, Nan?" Small pieces of chocolate flew from Billy's mouth as he spoke.

"Some people prefer sweets and others enjoy savoury foods. I enjoy fruit. I am more than happy with my apple."

Nan waved her apple in the air, holding it towards the light to show off its shine, turning it around, as if it were a diamond.

"This is why I am so thin and you are so tubby."

Nan was so thin, you could see her bones through her skin. Her glasses were too large for her face and her clothes looked like they would fit Billy as they were too big for her.

"Boring, boring," Billy chanted.

"Enough of your cheekiness, Billy. You had best get yourself off to school, otherwise you will be late," Nan insisted.

"Yes, I had better run. I must stop at the shop, to buy some more chocolate on the way to school." Billy shovelled the last remaining chocolate caramel into his mouth and then ran out of the door… well, he ran into the door as he tried to go through the door which wasn't open. "Ouch!" Billy cried.

Chapter two

The local shop

Friday 13th

When Billy got to the local shop, he saw three police cars parked outside. The owner, Mrs Barrett, was sitting on the pavement, crying and talking to a local Police Community Support Officer.

"Why are you crying?" Billy asked.

"Oh, Billy. My shop was robbed last night." Mrs Barrett blew her nose on the end of her sleeve.

"Oh no, that's awful. What did they take?"

"Chocolate." Mrs Barrett sniffled. Mrs Barrett's accent was very Welsh and very difficult to understand sometimes, and it was even more difficult now that she was crying.

"Chocolate?" Billy sounded confused. "You want some chocolate?"

"No, silly, that is what was taken – chocolate." Mrs Barrett wiped her nose on the other sleeve.

"Did they take anything else?" Billy tried to take a look inside the shop that was sealed off with police tape, just like in the movies.

"No, that is the strange thing. I have lots of very expensive items in my shop, I have – iPhones, kettles, toasters and all the takings from the till. They took nothing else, just chocolate."

"Wow." Billy paused. "That is very strange. How much chocolate?" Billy was starting to feel worried.

"All of it. Every last bar and bag. There is no chocolate left. Even my secret stash under the till I keep for emergency situations has all gone."

Billy hugged Mrs Barrett and cried with her.

"Do you have a piece of chocolate I can have, please, Billy?" Mrs Barrett broke the hug.

"No, sorry. I was coming to see you to buy some more before school."

"That is a shame. I could do with some right now."

"I will buy some at school and bring it to you on my way home, as I ate my last chocolate caramel before breakfast. Can you wait that long?"

"I will have to, Billy. That is very kind of you. Thank you." Mrs Barrett gave Billy another hug.

"Bye, Mrs Barrett, I will see you after school." Billy turned and shuffled slowly along in the direction of Marshmallow Junior School.

Chapter three

Mr Smith

Friday 13th

At school, all the children were talking about the local shop and the burglary.

"Tubby!" Cassandra shouted. She always called him that; most of the children called him that, due to the amount of chocolate he ate every day. "Did you steal the chocolate from Barrett's shop?"

"Of course I didn't!" Billy replied.

"You are always eating chocolate, so it must have been you." Cassandra smirked.

"Why would I do that? I have no chocolate to eat today, because someone stole it all from Mrs Barrett's shop and that someone was

not me," Billy shouted even louder.

The bell sounded for school to start and the children slowly walked to class. Everyone was still talking about the excitement of the overnight chocolate burglary.

Mr Smith gave Billy a strange look. "Have you got any chocolate, Billy?"

"No, sorry, sir. Why do you ask?" Billy was confused.

"Because someone has broken into the local shop and stolen all of the chocolate, and you are the main suspect," Mr Smith advised.

"Why does everyone keep accusing me? I am without chocolate today and that makes me sad, so very sad." Billy started to sniffle.

Chapter four

Nan's apples

Friday 13th

Billy's nan was watching the news on the television. Mrs Barrett was crying outside her shop. She was talking to the camera.

"It is a terrible tragedy that someone has stolen all my chocolate."

"Mrs Barrett," the reporter said, "do you have any idea who could have burgled your shop last night?"

Mrs Barrett shook her head and cried into her sleeve.

"What would you like to say to the thief?" the reporter asked.

Mrs Barrett turned to face the camera and made her plea. "If you have my chocolate, please bring it back. If you know who has stolen my chocolate, please phone the police. I have no chocolate to sell to all the children that come into my shop every day." She blew her nose on her sleeve.

"Silly woman," Nan muttered to herself. "It is only chocolate. Anyone would think that someone has stolen her pet dog."

Nan took a long slurp from her cup of tea and tucked into a large apple. Her favourite variety is Golden Delicious, but she would have to make do with a Gala until she went to the shop to buy some Golden Delicious apples.

She decided to walk and visit Mrs Barrett on the way to see if she was okay after her robbery last night.

Chapter five

Billy's favourite dinner

Friday 13th

Billy came home from school later than normal.

He was looking very sad.

"Hello, Billy, did you have a good day at school?"

Nan asked.

Billy didn't reply.

"Billy, is there something the matter?" Nan was

concerned.

"Someone stole all Mrs Barrett's chocolate. I have

not eaten any chocolate since breakfast." Billy

sobbed.

"Yes, I saw Mrs Barrett crying on the news at

lunchtime.

She was very upset," Nan commented.

"She is also very confused as the thieves only stole chocolate and left expensive items and all the money in the till."

"Very strange," Nan agreed. "Can I offer you a nice juicy apple, instead of chocolate?" Nan held a Golden Delicious to Billy's face.

"Yuck!" Billy screamed. "I want chocolate." Billy ran upstairs to his bedroom and slammed his door, very loudly.

"He still misses his mum," Nan muttered. Billy came to live with his nan when his mum became too ill to look after him. She now lives in a care home where nurses can look after her, as she is unable to look after herself. Billy visits his mum every Saturday, taking a big bag of chocolates with him, to give to her, to cheer her up.

Nan went to the kitchen to finish making Billy's favourite dinner.

"Dinner," Nan called to Billy up the stairs.

"I am not hungry!"

"But it is your favourite, Billy. I made it especially for you, as I know how upset you are."

"I am not interested!" Billy cried.

"It's triple-chocolate beef chilli," Nan tempted. "Chocolate cake for pudding, with chocolate custard and a large chocolate milkshake." Nan tried her hardest to get Billy to come to the dinner table. "It will go cold and to waste."

Billy shuffled down the stairs as if he were not interested, but soon sat at the dinner table and ate the entire chilli, then the pudding, and drank every last drop of the milkshake. Billy let out a loud burp.

"Excuse me." Billy waved his hand over his face.

"Thank you, Nan, that was amazing. What are you having for dinner?"

"I too am having my favourite dinner: stuffed apples followed by apple pie with a large glass of apple juice." Nan smiled.

"Yuck, you really are weird – you only eat apples." Billy grimaced.

"Yes, I do, but remember all you eat is chocolate. That is not normal either," Nan said.

"Thank you for dinner, Nan. I am going to go to bed now, I am feeling very tired." Billy turned and walked towards the stairs.

"Night, Billy. You get some rest and hopefully, whilst you are sleeping, the police will find out who stole Mrs Barrett's chocolate."

"I hope so. I feel so bad for her." Billy sighed.

"Well don't worry about Mrs Barrett. She will be okay, I am sure."

Chapter six

The police

Saturday 14th

Billy was woken by a loud banging on the front door. Someone was desperate to wake him.

Billy stumbled down the stairs in his pyjamas and tripped over his dressing gown belt, rolled down the last three stairs and landed with a loud thud. Billy screamed out. "Ouch, that hurt." The banging on the door got louder. Billy crawled to the front door and called, "Who is it?"

"The police," came a stern reply from the other side of the door. "Are you okay?"

"I am okay, give me a minute, I am just getting up off the floor." Billy gritted his teeth through the pain. Billy reached for the door handle, and held his head in pain as he opened the door.

"Billy Jenkins?" the officer asked.

"Yes, please come in. I need to sit down and put an ice pack on my head. I just fell down the stairs trying to answer the door quickly."

The officer stood in the living room and towered above Billy. The officer as tall as a giraffe.

"Hello, Billy. I am PCSO Todd Austin. I am here to talk to you about the theft at the local shop. Do you know anything about it?"

"No, nothing. Why are you asking me?" Billy looked confused.

"We are asking everyone in the local area," the very tall PCSO said.

"Well, I am sorry, I don't know anything. All I know is that I couldn't buy any chocolate on the way to school and I love chocolate." Billy reached for a screwed-up tissue from his dressing gown pocket and blew his nose.

"Yes, that is what people are telling me, that you love chocolate," PCSO Austin said.

"Do I need a lawyer?" Billy asked.

"Why would you need a lawyer?"

"That is what they say in all the movies when a policeman comes to quiz someone, isn't it?"

"This isn't a movie, this is a very serious crime." The PCSO was not amused by Billy's comment. "Mrs Barrett has had her shop broken into and all of the chocolate was stolen – nothing else, just chocolate. Do you not think that is rather strange?"

"Yes, it is, but as I said, I couldn't buy any chocolate on the way to school and I love chocolate."

"Okay, thank you for your time, Billy, and I am sorry to wake you this early on a Saturday morning. If you hear anything, please can you call me." The very tall PCSO offered Billy his card. "Is your mum in?"

"No, she doesn't live here."

"Your dad then?"

"No, sorry, he left us, when I was a baby."

"Oh, I am sorry to hear that. Who looks after you then?"

"My nan. She is in bed, she sleeps through everything." Billy laughed.

"Super, as long as you are okay." The very tall PCSO now looked concerned.

"Yes, thank you. I am just in a little pain, because of the bang to my head." Billy held his head as if it were going to fall off.

"Well, thank you for your time. I am sorry to wake you so early and I am sorry you fell down the stairs to answer the door to me. I will see myself out." PCSO Austin turned and left.

Billy walked unsteadily to the kitchen and took a handful of ice from the freezer, wrapped it in a tea towel and placed the handmade ice pack on his sore head.

"Who was that?" Billy's nan was standing in the doorway.

Billy jumped. "Wow, Nan, I wasn't expecting you to be standing there."

"Are you okay? What have you done to your head?" Billy's nan looked concerned.

"I fell down the stairs, rushing to answer the door, which was being banged very loudly."

"I heard the door. It sounded like someone trying to break in. Who was it?"

"It was a very tall PCSO, asking me about Mrs Barrett's chocolate robbery."

"What did you say?"

"I told him that I do not know anything. He did give me his card and asked me to call him if I hear anything." Billy handed the card to his nan.

PCSO Todd Austin

Billy's nan studied the card. "I will file this away, you never know when you might need it." She put the card in the top kitchen drawer, the drawer that contained lots of useless stuff. There was sticky tape, where you couldn't find the end. A ball of string that was so unwound, it was no longer a ball of string. Batteries no one was really sure worked. Birthday candles that had only been lit once. Lots of takeaway menus that had never been looked at. All of the useless stuff stayed in the drawer as it may become useful one day.

Chapter seven

The visit to Mum

Saturday 14th

Billy dressed in his best clothes as he did every Saturday for his visit to his mum in the care home.

"Are you ready?" Nan called.

"Yes," Billy mumbled.

"Why are you so sad? You are going to see your mum."

"I don't have any chocolate to take with me, as Mrs Barrett's shop was broken into."

"I am sure your mum won't mind. It's you she wants to see, not the chocolate." Nan tried to calm Billy.

"Yes, but I have taken chocolate to her every week that I have visited."

"Let's go and see your mum now. Get your coat, Billy." Nan put on her coat and soon they were both ready to leave.

Billy sat quietly in the car all the way to the nursing home. He wasn't his normal chatty self.

"Are you not looking forward to seeing your mum today?"

"Of course I am. I am just worried what she will say when she sees me without a huge bag of chocolate." Billy started to cry.

"Well, we are here now, let's go and see your mum." Nan got out of the car and waited for Billy to emerge slowly.

Mum was sitting in her favourite chair in the day room, watching the television.

"Billy!" Mum shouted when she saw him come in the door. "Come and give your mum a big hug."

Billy walked slowly towards his mum.

"Billy, you look upset, what is the matter?"

"Mrs Barrett's shop was broken into and all her chocolate was stolen, so I couldn't bring you any chocolate today. I am so sorry." Billy sniffed.

"Oh, Billy, it is not the chocolate I want to see, it is you." Mum gave him a huge squeeze.

"I did tell him that," Nan said.

"Yes, but I still feel bad." Billy sighed.

"Tell me about the break-in at the shop?" Mum asked.

"I went to school yesterday and I saw Mrs Barrett on the pavement, crying, and there were police officers, everywhere, just like in the movies. She said that her shop was broken into overnight."

"How sad for her. Did they take much?"

"That is the strangest thing – all they took was her chocolate. They didn't touch the electrical items or the sweets, just the chocolate."

"Wow, someone likes chocolate then." Mum seemed surprised.

"That is the awful thing – everyone at school thought it was me, as I like chocolate so much."

"Oh, Billy, I wouldn't worry, children can be horrible sometimes, in the words they use," Mum reassured him.

"Even Mr Smith, the headteacher, accused me of stealing the chocolate."

"Really? That is awful. What did he say?" Mum quizzed.

"He asked if I had any chocolate, as someone broke into the shop overnight." Billy wiped his nose, which was starting to run, on his sleeve.

"Oh, Billy, I wouldn't worry. You know that you didn't do it, that's all that matters. Tell me something good that has happened to you this week instead." Mum tried to change the subject.

Billy and his nan stayed chatting with Billy's mum for two hours. The care staff announced that it was time for lunch. Billy gave his mum a huge cuddle and kissed her on both cheeks.

"Bye, Mum. I promise I will bring you some chocolate when I visit next week."

"Thanks, Billy. It's you I want to see, not the chocolate."

Billy and Nan both waved goodbye.

Chapter eight

The tuck shop

Monday 16th

Billy turned the corner and could see his school ahead of him. There seemed to be a lot of activity outside: four police cars and lots of police officers and PCSOs. There were several police dogs sniffing in the hedges and the playing fields. There was also police tape across the entrance to the school.

When Billy got closer, everyone started pointing to him and calling out his nickname. "Tubby." The police dogs started pulling on their leads, wanting to run towards him. Billy didn't know whether to run or stay still; the dogs were frightening him.

"Billy Jenkins?" a policeman called out. The dog he was holding looked eager to run towards Billy.

"Yes." Billy trembled.

"I am PC Brown and this is my dog, Biscuit. I need to ask you a few questions, please?" The policeman started walking towards Billy, with his dog on the lead.

"Yes, of course." Billy was trembling more and more. "Can you put the dog away, please?"

"Of course I can. Biscuit, come with me." The policeman put Biscuit back

into his van.

"Thank you." Billy sighed with relief.

"Now, Billy, the school tuck shop was broken into last night."

Billy started to cry. "What did they take?"

"They stole chocolate. That is all they took, every last bar of it."

"That is awful." Billy almost fell over as he felt dizzy and had to sit down on the pavement.

"Do you know anything about this, Billy?" the very large policeman asked.

"No, the first time I heard the news is when you told me." Billy was shaking now.

"Okay, we are asking all the children that attend the school if they have seen or heard anything," said PC Brown.

"Where will I buy my chocolate from now? I have none with me today. First, Mrs Barrett's shop and now the school tuck shop."

"So, you like chocolate then, Billy?"

"Of course, don't all children?" Billy was confused by the policeman's question.

"Not all children like chocolate. My son likes crisps more than chocolate – salt and vinegar are his favourite. He doesn't care for chocolate at all."

"Wow, that is weird. Crisps do not taste anything like chocolate."

"That is why, Billy, everyone is asking you if you know anything, as you like chocolate so much," PC Brown told him.

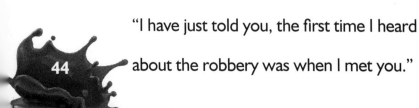

"I have just told you, the first time I heard about the robbery was when I met you."

"Okay, thank you, I understand. Anyway, the good news is that the school is closed today, so you can go home."

"Wow, that is awesome." Billy paused and thought about his reply. "I am pleased about the day off, I mean, not about the tuck shop robbery." Billy started to feel embarrassed as he thought his response could make the very large policeman think he was the chocolate thief.

45

Billy ran home, flew through the front door and startled his nan.

"Wow, Billy, are you okay? Are you ill? Why are you home early?" Billy's nan asked lots of questions.

"No, I am not ill. School is shut today."

"Oh no, why is the school shut?" Nan asked.

"Because someone robbed the school tuck shop last night and has stolen all the chocolate. There are police and police dogs searching the school and the school grounds." Billy didn't stop for a breath as he was explaining the events to his nan.

"Oh my gosh, that is awful. First Mrs Barrett's shop and now the school tuck shop."

"It is awful. Even more awful is that everyone is blaming me for the robberies. Just because I like eating chocolate, everyone thinks I have stolen it."

"That is very unfair, Billy. Just because you like to eat chocolate."

"Other children like chocolate too, apart from the policeman's son, who has a dog called Biscuit."

"Why, does he like biscuits?" Nan asked.

"No, he would rather eat crisps, salt and vinegar in particular."

"Well, I like apples and I don't like chocolate." Nan waved an apple in the air.

"Yes, Nan, apples are not even a treat, they are just weird." Billy twirled his fingers around his head to signal weird.

"Enough of your cheek, young man."

"Sorry, Nan." Billy looked down as he had been told off.

"Well, if there is no school, maybe we should go out for the day," Nan suggested.

"Excellent idea, Nan. Where shall we go?"

"I am sure I will think of something, somewhere that has chocolate milkshakes and games to play." Nan grabbed her coat.

"Thank you, just let me get changed, out of my school uniform." Billy rushed off upstairs to get changed.

Chapter nine

School assembly

Tuesday 17th

Everyone was very quiet at school. There was no shouting or laughing in the school playground and no one was playing football.

A sign on the tuck shop read:

Tuck shop closed until further notice

Billy started to sniffle as he read the sign.

The whole school was called into assembly immediately. Mr Smith, the headteacher, was standing with his arms crossed and he was looking very angry.

"Good morning, children."

"Good morning, Mr Smith," the children all replied together.

"Now, children, I am sure you have all heard the very shocking news that yesterday when I arrived into school, I found the tuck shop had been broken into and all of the chocolate had been stolen." Mr Smith's voice was raised.

All the children gasped.

"All the chocolate had been stolen, every last bar," Mr Smith said. "No sweets, drinks or crisps were stolen, just chocolate – and all of it."

The children gasped again.

"If anyone has any information as to who may be responsible for this crime, then they can come to me in my office, at any time."

The children sat very still and very quiet.

"The police," Mr Smith said, "are concerned that this robbery is very similar to the robbery at Mrs Barrett's shop last week."

A few of the children started whispering amongst themselves.

"Attention!" Mr Smith shouted. "If you have something to say, you can come to my office."

The children stopped talking immediately.

"Everyone, back to class, quickly as you can."

Mr Smith turned and marched out of the assembly hall.

The children gathered their coats and bags and hurried back to class in silence.

Billy wasn't looking where he was going and he walked straight into Mr Smith.

"Mr Jenkins." Mr Smith sounded very angry.

"My office."

"Yes, sir, when would you like me to come to your office?"

"Now!" Mr Smith shouted and walked off.

Billy followed slowly behind. He was not looking

forward to being told off by Mr Smith.

"Hurry, boy, I have not got all day."

"Yes, sir." Billy hurried his pace.

Billy stood in Mr Smith's office. He did not know

where to put his eyes.

"Take your hands out of your pockets, boy. Stand tall."

"Yes, sir." Billy quickly removed his hands and stood to attention.

"Now, Billy, do you know anything about the tuck shop robbery?"

"No, sir, nothing."

"Okay, if you hear anything, please come and see me."

"Yes, sir, I will, but I know absolutely nothing."

"Maybe at the moment, but children talk. It is just a case of waiting until they do."

"You want me to be your spy?" Billy looked confused.

"No, not a spy, just reporting to me the truth about this awful situation."

"Why does everyone think I know anything about the robberies?" Billy sobbed.

"You like chocolate, Billy, don't you?" Mr Smith asked.

"Yes, but I am not going to steal it. If I did, then I wouldn't have any to buy every day. Why would I steal it?"

"Because you can eat it all?" Mr Smith quizzed.

"Well, I am as sad as you, as I haven't eaten any chocolate for days now as someone has robbed the local shop and now the school tuck shop."

"Billy, get back to class."

"Yes, sir."

"Hurry, you are now late for your lesson."

Billy gathered his coat and bag and ran out of the door. He sneaked into the class as quietly as he could, hoping that no one would notice he arrived late. All the children did notice his late arrival. Billy blushed brightly.

Chapter ten

Billy's favourite café

Tuesday 17th

Billy was so sad when he got home from school.

"What is the matter, Billy?" Nan asked.

"I have been blamed all day, for the theft of the

chocolate from the tuck shop."

"Don't listen to them, lad. They have nothing else

to do with their lives."

"Nan, that is easy for you to say, you are not at

school with these people – even the headteacher

called me into his office and questioned me."

Billy sniffled and wiped his nose on his sleeve.

"I'm sure no one blames you, Billy," Nan said

whilst giving Billy a huge hug.

"They do, all of them. No one understands that I wouldn't steal all the chocolate. I like chocolate so much and I can't buy any if it has all been stolen."

"What have the police said about the break-in?" Nan was concerned.

"No one is saying anything apart from that I must have done it."

"Please don't let them get to you. How about I take you to your favourite café and buy you the largest chocolate milkshake?"

"I am not sure I feel up to it today, Nan."

"Oh, Billy, you are really sad. Please put your coat on and we will go and have some fun."

Billy walked slowly to his room and came down a few minutes later with his coat.

Billy and his nan sat by the window of their favourite café. Everyone was talking about the tuck shop robbery. Billy put his fingers in his ears to block out all of the excitement that everyone was talking about.

"Billy, would you like anything to eat?" Nan broke Billy's silence.

"I suppose so," Billy mumbled.

"What would you like?"

"I'm not sure, you can order for me."

"I'm sure once you have had some food,

you will feel much better, then afterward we can go to the shops and get you a new game for your PlayStation if you wish?"

"Thank you, Nan, you are the best." Billy leaned over the table and gave his nan a huge kiss on the cheek.

The waitress brought over the biggest plate of burger and chips for Billy. She placed it in the middle of the table.

"Wow, I won't eat all of that on my own." Billy's eyes widened.

"No, we can share, as I wouldn't eat it all on my own either."

They both ate in silence and enjoyed the huge plate of burger and chips. Once they had finished, Billy got up and went to the toilet.

When he returned, Nan was talking to the waitress about the break-in at the school tuck shop.

"My sister goes to the same school," the waitress said. "She was so upset by the school tuck shop being broken into. She came home in floods of tears."

"I am sure they will catch the burglar soon. If they don't, the town will completely run out of chocolate and then what are we going to do?"

"Move to another town perhaps?" The waitress laughed.

Billy wasn't laughing.

"Sorry, that wasn't funny." The waitress turned a bright red colour.

"Thank you for the food, it was lovely." Billy shook the hand of the waitress. "Bye for now and have a good day." Billy turned and left the café and his nan followed slowly behind.

"Which shop shall we go to?" Nan asked, trying to cheer Billy up.

"I am not sure. There are only a few that have a good selection."

"Follow me." Nan grabbed Billy's arm and pulled him along the road to the nearest game shop. Once inside there was a buzz and everyone was talking about the recent chocolate robberies.

"Everywhere we go, it's all everyone is talking about." Billy looked around uncomfortably. "Can we just get a game and go, please, Nan?"

"Of course. If you go and pick a game, I can pay for it and you can wait outside if you are feeling uncomfortable."

"Thanks, Nan." Billy picked up the first game that he didn't have already, handed it to his nan and walked out of the shop.

Chapter eleven

Looking for the thief

Tuesday 17th

Billy wanted to go to bed early. "Are you tired?"

Nan asked.

"Yes, I have had a busy day. I hope you do not

mind?" Billy climbed the stairs.

"Of course I don't mind. You go and get some

rest."

Billy got straight into bed. Nan thought he was

tired, but he had other plans for the evening. He

had decided he would wake up at two o'clock in

the morning and go out all dressed in black and see

if he could find the chocolate thief.

Billy's alarm woke him at two o'clock. He felt very tired, but he had already decided he would go out and see if he could find the thief. He got dressed in his black tracksuit bottoms, a black T-shirt, a black jumper, black trainers, a black coat and black hat. "No one should be able to see me, dressed in these clothes," Billy whispered to himself.

It was very cold outside. "Why would any robbers want to be out at this time of the night? It is freezing," Billy commented as he walked the streets. He saw a security van drive up the road and he hid behind a wheelie bin so he couldn't be seen. "That was close," he whispered.

He then walked past all the shops and looked inside all the windows to see if there was anyone in there. The shops were empty. Billy thought this strange: the robbers had been out every night but tonight there was no one.

Billy felt a hand on his shoulder and he screamed really loudly.

"What are you doing, son?" a deep voice asked.

"Nothing. Who are you?" Billy's voice was shaking.

"I asked you first. What are you doing, son?"

"I am looking for the chocolate thief. What are you doing?" Billy was too scared to turn around and face the voice that was talking to him.

"I am taking you to the police station, son," the deep voice stated.

"No, please, please don't. I am only looking for the chocolate thief," Billy pleaded.

"Likely story, son." The deep voice turned Billy round to him and showed his large face. He was wearing a police uniform.

"Get in my police car, now!" the policeman shouted.

Billy was very scared and did not argue with the policeman.

At the police station, the police man helped Billy from the car. Billy was shaking from his head to his feet. The policeman walked Billy into the police station. There was a policeman behind the desk and he looked rather strangely at the policeman and Billy as they came through the door.

"What do we have here?" the policeman asked.

"I caught him looking in shop windows," the policeman replied.

"Oh dear, why are you out at this time in the morning, young man?" the policeman quizzed.

Billy was crying. "I am looking for the chocolate thief." Billy sniffled.

"That is why we have police to look for thieves. You do not need to worry about such matters." The policeman seemed angry.

"I am very sorry," Billy replied. "I was only trying to help."

"Thank you, but I must phone your parents to let them know you are out at three o'clock in the morning, dressed in black, looking for a chocolate thief." The policeman was getting angrier.

"I live with my nan. My mum lives in a care home." Billy continued to cry.

"What is your name, son?" the policeman asked.

"Billy Jenkins."

"Okay, Billy, can you give me the telephone number for your nan and I will have to call her now."

Billy gave the number to the policeman and waited for the policeman to return after he phoned his nan. "Nan is going to be so angry."

The policeman returned a few minutes later. "Your nan is on her way. You can wait over there." The policeman pointed to a broken plastic chair.

After thirty minutes, Billy's nan turned up, in her pyjamas and pink fluffy dressing gown. "Billy, what were you thinking?"

"I am so sorry, Nan. I just wanted to catch the chocolate thief." Billy was crying even more now.

"You don't need to do that. Come on, let's get you home."

"Am I in trouble?" Billy asked.

"Not this time. You are lucky the police didn't want to do anything other than make a phone call to me. Say sorry to the policeman."

Billy turned to the policeman. "I am sorry."

"Thank you for your apology. Please, you do not need to worry about trying to find the chocolate thief – that is our job. I promise we are working, very hard, to find the robber."

Chapter twelve

The local news

Wednesday 18th

Once his nan had driven him home, Billy made a hot chocolate and went to bed, but he never went back to sleep. He went to school looking very tired.

"Wow, Billy, are you ill?" Mr Stuart asked.

"No," Billy replied. "I just didn't sleep too well last night," he lied.

"I am pleased to hear that. I don't want you being sick in my science class."

Billy was glad he wasn't feeling sick, as Mr Stuart was not showing any signs of sympathy.

The remainder of the day went by in a haze as Billy was so tired from the night time, and he was pleased to be going home when the final bell went. He walked home very slowly; he was still low on energy.

When Billy arrived home, there were television cameras outside his house. "Very strange, what has happened now?" Billy was feeling scared. "Did they find out about me going out last night?" Billy wondered.

Billy opened the door and called out, "Nan, are you here?"

Nan appeared from behind the sofa.

"What are you doing behind the sofa?" Billy asked.

"Them television crew people, they keep peering in the windows and knocking the door, asking if they can interview me."

"Why?"

"I have no idea. Now you are home, they are probably going to start knocking again." Nan was shaking as she was talking.

There was a loud knock on the door. "Mr Jenkins, are you in there?"

"Of course I am in here, you saw me come in." Billy muttered through gritted teeth.

The knocking got louder and louder. Billy gave up

and opened the door. "Can I help you?"

"I would like to ask if you would like to be

included in the documentary we are making."

The television producer rambled on. "We are

looking for children that love chocolate and those

that have been affected by the recent chocolate

robberies. Can I ask if you can be included, please,

Mr Jenkins?"

"I suppose so. I do like chocolate and I am so

upset that all the chocolate in this town is being

robbed and there is none left for me to buy." Billy

brightened up his voice.

"Great, thank you, Mr Jenkins. Can we start now?"

"I suppose so." Billy opened the door to

let the television crew in.

"Thank you so much, Billy. Can I call you 'Billy'?"

"Yes, you can," Billy replied.

"Excellent. I am Maria and the man on the microphone is Mike – very funny really, Mike who looks after the microphone – and June is behind the camera." Mike and June both waved hello to Billy.

"So, Billy, please tell me, what are your thoughts regarding the chocolate robberies?" Maria asked.

"I am very sad, obviously. I have no chocolate left to buy and I love chocolate."

"Do you have any idea who may be behind the robberies?"

"No, not at all. I went out last night to look for the robber, but I could not see anyone."

"You went out last night?" Maria quizzed.

"Yes, it wasn't very successful. A policeman found me looking in shop windows. I got taken to the police station and my nan had to come and pick me up," Billy replied.

"Did the police think that you are the chocolate thief?" Maria was getting excited now.

"No, they just said I was silly for going out alone, looking for a thief, when it is their job to do that."

"Well, Billy, if I were the police, I would think that you were out looking for more chocolate to rob."

"Thankfully, you are not the police. I was stupid, but I am so sad that there is someone out there robbing all the chocolate in this town and I and other children cannot buy any."

"Well, thank you, Billy, for your time. I think we have enough footage to be going on with." Maria turned to leave. "If you do hear anything about who may be behind these robberies, would you mind calling me?" Maria handed Billy her card.

"Of course, thank you." Billy closed the door behind them.

"They were not expecting you to say that," Nan commented.

"What?" Billy quizzed.

"That you went out looking for the robber last night," Nan reminded him.

"Oh, that. At least they can leave me alone now. I am very tired and want to go to bed for a sleep for a while." Billy climbed the stairs to bed.

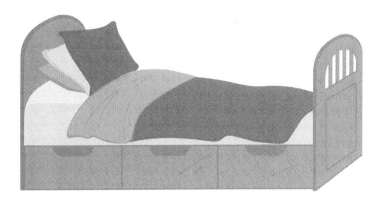

Chapter thirteen

Rationing

Saturday 21st

Billy woke up and shuffled down the stairs as he was still very tired. Nan was glued to the breakfast television channel. The reporter was looking sad as she spoke.

"With the recent robberies of chocolate in the town, the shops are now rationing the amount of chocolate that one person can buy at any one time."

"No!" Billy screamed at the television as if the television presenter could hear him.

"The chocolate factories cannot keep up with the demand the town's residents are putting

on them. Once the chocolate gets delivered to the shops, a thief is taking all the chocolate." The television presenter was almost crying. "It is my daughter's birthday party at the weekend and I cannot buy enough chocolates to put in her party bags. She is going to be so upset."

"They need to stop this thief!" Billy screamed at the television again.

"The police are doing everything they can to catch the robber. They have extra patrols on the streets at nights. The police can confirm, they did catch someone looking in shop windows three nights ago, but it was found to be unrelated to the robberies." the television presenter went on.

"I think they mean you, Billy." Nan gasped.

"Thankfully, they didn't mention it was a silly

child looking for the thief," Billy acknowledged.

"Everyone would think it was me."

"But it was you," Nan replied.

"Yes, but I don't want anyone knowing it was me. I

will look even more suspicious than I already am."

"The rationing is going to be five-hundred grams

of chocolate per day, per person." The television

presenter sobbed some more.

"Five-hundred grams." Billy gasped. "That is only one sitting of chocolate for me. What am I going to do about the rest of the day?" Billy started to sniffle.

"Please don't worry, Billy. They will catch the thief soon, I am sure of it. Then you will be able to go back to buying chocolate again." Nan tried to calm Billy and stop him crying.

Billy stormed upstairs and slammed the bedroom door shut, very loudly.

Nan called Billy for his dinner. Sitting on the table was a steaming hot plate of chocolate pasta.

"There is chocolate steamed-pudding for afters," Nan said cheerily.

"Thanks, Nan, but I am not sure if I am that hungry," Billy mumbled.

"Chocolate will make you feel better, it always does in times of trouble."

"Yes, but shouldn't we be rationing our chocolate supply?" Billy asked.

"Oh, don't worry, Billy. It is only one meal and you are very upset and you deserve cheering up."

Billy ate all of his meal and enjoyed it very much.

Billy dragged himself slowly from the table. "I am going to go out and see if the television presenter is telling the truth and see how many shops are rationing their chocolate supply."

"Would you like me to come with you?" Nan asked brightly.

"No, Nan, you are okay. I am not sure how long I will be out for. You will get bored." Billy grabbed his coat.

Outside the shops there was a sea of police vehicles and television reporters. Billy saw the police officer that took him to the police station.

"Billy Jenkins, what are you doing here?"

"I have heard that chocolate is being rationed. I wanted to see if it was true," Billy replied.

"Well, it is, now please keep yourself out of mischief. We are doing everything we can to find the chocolate thief – we do not need other people getting in the way." The police officer stood very tall as he spoke.

"Sorry, sir, I am just seeing if I can buy any chocolate anywhere."

"I don't think so, son. If I was you, I would run on home."

Billy turned and walked home slowly.

Billy threw the front door open and stormed upstairs, very upset.

"Billy," Nan called after him. "Why are you upset?"

"It is true, Nan," Billy called down the stairs.

"There are police everywhere in town and there is no chocolate to buy, anywhere."

"I have some chocolate in the back of the cupboard, I will find you some."

Billy took the large chocolate bar of fruit and nut and went back up to his room. He ate the whole bar, with just three mouthfuls. He felt much better and then went to sleep, more contented than he had been for a few days.

Chapter fourteen

The leak

Monday 23rd

Billy slowly walked downstairs, yawning. He was ready in his school uniform.

"You look tired, Billy," Nan said.

"I am very tired. I hardly slept all weekend. I have been worrying about the chocolate rationing."

"I would not lose sleep over something so trivial," Nan remarked.

"It is certainly not trivial!" Billy screamed.

"Okay, I can see you are upset, but it is only chocolate."

"Only chocolate… my favourite food in the whole world. How am I going to survive?" Billy cried.

"You will survive, because we are human beings and that is what we do, we learn to survive in times of crisis," Nan replied as a matter of fact.

"This is not the 1940s, Nan. This is the twenty-first century." Billy grabbed a slice of toast from the table, covered it in a thick helping of chocolate spread and stormed off to school.

On the walk to school, Billy went into every shop that sold chocolate and every shop had a sign up saying: Sorry, no chocolate.

Billy started to cry inside. He didn't want any of his schoolmates to see him crying. It is only chocolate after all – they would tease him.

On arrival at school, Billy saw the tuck shop had a sign saying:

Chocolate rationing no chocolate on sale.

There was excitement amongst everyone.

"What is happening?" Billy asked another student.

"There is a rumour that the chocolate factory has a leak."

"A leak? What sort of leak?"

"A chocolate leak. They think someone has laid a pipe from the chocolate factory to somewhere else," the other student said.

"That is outrageous! How can someone lay a pipe from the chocolate factory?" Billy was confused.

"This is what all the fuss is about. Everyone is very confused. The police are now searching through the homes of everyone who works at the chocolate factory," the other student explained.

The bell sounded for assembly. All the students shuffled into the hall and sat down, but there was a constant murmur as everyone was talking about the news about the chocolate factory.

"Quiet please!" Mr Smith shouted. "Good morning, everyone."

"Good morning, Mr Smith," everyone replied together and then stopped talking immediately, for fear of being put on report for talking during assembly.

"Now, I am sure most of you have heard the chocolate factory has been reported as having a leak. Now this is old news, I hope not to hear another word on the subject. This whole story of the chocolate thief is becoming very annoying now."

All the children were stunned.

"Can you all get back to schoolwork now, please? I know that the local news is exciting, but this really has taken away your attention from the school curriculum and I would now like you all to refocus on your studies. That is why you are all here after all. Do I have your co-operation?"

"Yes, sir," everyone replied.

"Louder!" Mr Smith shouted.

Everyone replied, louder, "Yes, sir."

"Thank you. Now, on to class, quietly and quickly as you can, please." Mr Smith turned and left the hall in a hurry.

The rest of the school day was very dull and boring for Billy and he was very upset that he did not have any chocolate to eat all day.

When Billy arrived home, Nan was busy preparing dinner.

"Hi, Nan," Billy said.

"Hi Billy, how was school today?"

"Pretty awful really," Billy mumbled.

"Oh, why is that?"

"Mr Smith banned us all from talking about the chocolate thief."

"Wow, why is that then?" Nan queried.

"There was news about the chocolate factory having a leak and everyone was talking about it and Mr Smith said it is old news and we need to get back to our studies."

"He has a good point – you are at school to study."

"Is it true then, about the leak from the chocolate factory?"

"Yes, very true, it is all over the news."

"Really?"

"Yes, the police have been everywhere – also I have heard helicopters overhead all day."

"I need to go and watch the news." Billy ran off towards the television.

Every news channel was reporting on the same story.

"Breaking news. Chocolate factory has a leak."
There was police tape all across the front of the
building and there were many, many police cars
and vans. There were also three fire engines and
over the voice of the reporter there was the sound
of a helicopter. The reporter had to shout to be
heard.

"A worker in the chocolate factory, Devine Prime behind me, discovered a leak today. The leak is coming from the main chocolate pipe that is used to make the chocolate treats that they produce here. The fire brigade is currently investigating the source of the leak and the police are currently interviewing all of the factory workers. At the moment, there is nothing more to report."

Billy stood staring at the television, open-mouthed, shocked by what the reporter was saying.

"Nan, how can this be?" Billy called.

"I have no idea, Billy."

"We are already being rationed, and now this – it is going to make things worse." Billy started to cry.

"I have a small stash of chocolate. Please don't tell anyone, but I always buy a few extra bars each week and put them away for emergencies," Nan explained.

"This is definitely an emergency. Where do you keep it?"

"Why don't you get changed and ready for dinner?"

"Thanks, Nan."

Chapter fifteen

The police search

Tuesday 24th

The television was still reporting on the same story.

"Devine Prime chocolate factory has a chocolate leak."

The reporter looked very sad as she spoke. Maybe not just about the chocolate leak, but maybe the fact it was raining very hard. She was standing in the same place as last night, in front of the factory. There were still many police cars, police vans, and fire engines. It looked as though no one had been home to bed all night.

"The police are still interviewing all the workers of the factory. The factory has over three-hundred workers, so it is going to take some time to interview them all. The fire brigade has secured the leak, but the production of chocolate has still been halted, whilst the investigations continue." The reporter's voice was getting quieter and quieter as she was struggling to find the words.

"The police have been able to confirm the leak was a deliberate act by someone to remove the chocolate from the factory. There is no more information at present, but the police are working hard to find the person or persons responsible for this savage attack. The owners of the chocolate factory, the Prime Brothers, were not available to comment on the situation, but they are obviously devastated."

"Oh my gosh, Nan, this is awful. They think someone has deliberately vandalised the chocolate factory. Why would someone do this?"

"I have no idea, Billy. The police will find out, I am sure. That is their job, after all. This trouble is affecting so many people's lives."

"I am dreading school again today. Everyone has been teasing me about the thefts already. I am going to get more accusations today, I am sure."

"Ignore them, Billy. You know you are not the thief, that's all that matters. If anyone teases you, you just remember that."

Billy went and got dressed for school.

As Billy approached the school gates, the roads were covered with police officers and their vehicles.

"What has happened now?" Billy asked one of the police officers.

"We are just investigating all lines of enquiry," the police officer informed him.

"What does that mean?"

"It means, young man, that I cannot tell you anything specific, apart from that we are investigating all lines of enquiry."

"Investigating here." Billy was shocked.

"Like I said, son, I cannot tell you any more information. Please run along to school, like a good boy, otherwise I will have to have you arrested for obstructing a police officer."

Billy ran as fast as he could towards the school gates.

The atmosphere inside the school was very tense.

Students were being searched as they entered the school.

"Next," a PCSO called.

Billy stepped forwards, very slowly, towards the PCSO.

"Hurry up, son, I have all the other pupils' bags to search."

Billy quickened his step and placed his school bag on the table in front of the PCSO.

"What are you searching for?" Billy enquired.

"That, my lad, is something I cannot tell you. If I told you, you could tell the whole school and then we wouldn't find the evidence we are looking for as they could destroy it first."

"Evidence in this school this sounds serious," Billy replied.

"It is serious, very serious in fact. There is a thief in our community. This thief is damaging lives and we must find him or her as soon as we can."

"I can assure you that the thief is not in my school bag unless he is very small."

"That is not very funny." The PCSO looked at Billy, with a very serious face.

"Sorry." Billy looked at the floor. "However, if he is that small, then maybe that is how they got into the chocolate factory."

"Leave the investigating to the police, that is what we are here for."

"Sorry," Billy said again.

"Next," the PCSO called to the queue of children, who were waiting for their turn to be searched.

Chapter sixteen

The arrest

Tuesday 24th

Billy was daydreaming about eating a huge bar of chocolate when he should have been answering questions from the maths teacher. Mr Anderson's lessons were always dull and very boring; Mr Anderson was from Denmark and his accent made it very difficult to understand. Billy looked out of the window and saw more police cars arrive rather hastily.

Out stepped two police officers and two men in

suits, who must have been detectives.

"What is going on now?" Billy muttered.

Soon after the police entered the school, they left

with Mr Smith in handcuffs.

"Mr Smith is in handcuffs!" Billy shouted to the rest

of the class.

The class all stopped what they were doing and

ran towards the window.

Even Mr Anderson joined the children and watched.

Mr Smith sat crying in the police cell, all alone. The

cell door opened.

"We will interview you now, Mr Smith. Please

come with me." The detective waited for Mr

Smith to get up from the uncomfortably hard bed.

He shuffled behind the police officer towards the

interview room.

Mr Smith sat fidgeting at the interview table,

twisting his hands in anticipation.

"Mr Smith, Gary – do you mind if I call you

'Gary'?" The detective asked.

Mr Smith nodded his head.

"The interview today is with Mr Smith, his solicitor Mr Porter, Detective Constable Hamilton and myself, Detective Inspector Gibson," DC Hamilton said.

"So, Gary, you have been arrested today on the suspicion of theft from the chocolate factory, Devine Prime. What do you have to say?"

Mr Smith looked at the floor. "No comment," Mr Smith replied.

The detective looked blankly at Mr Smith. "We have followed a pipe leading from the chocolate factory to your home address. How do you explain this?"

"No comment."

"You are a headteacher, Gary. Surely you have more vocabulary than 'no comment'?"

"No comment," Mr Smith said again.

"My colleagues are at your house right now, Gary. They are searching for evidence that you are the chocolate thief, the one that the whole town has been searching for. What will they find at your house, Gary?"

"No comment," Mr Smith replied once more.

"An educated man like yourself, turned into a serial thief – this is not the best example to set for the children at your school, is it?"

"No comment."

"Interview terminated." DI Gibson stood up sharply and kicked the chair. "Take him back to the cell!" DI Gibson shouted and left the room.

At Mr Smith's home, there were police everywhere. DI Gibson entered the house and the police were removing items from Mr Smith's home, searching for evidence.

"Have you found anything yet?" DI Gibson asked an officer.

"Nothing yet, sir," the police officer replied.

DI Gibson turned to leave in disgust when he heard a series of shouts from the other room, from the police officers that were searching the house. "Yes."

He ran into the other room and saw several officers taking a hammer to a wall.

"What is behind there, do you think?" DI Gibson asked.

"That is what we are about to find out. It must be something worth hiding," one of the officers said.

Once the wall had been destroyed all the police officers stood very still and stared, opened mouthed and silent, at the contents of the hidden room.

Before them were stacks and stacks of chocolate

boxes. So many boxes, they couldn't quite see

how many boxes there were. They started to

remove some boxes and they then discovered

a huge cooking pot, almost as big as the room,

overflowing with liquid chocolate and a pipe

leading from it.

"Bingo!" DI Gibson shouted. "I'm going back to
the police station, to nick the creep." He turned
and ran towards his car.

DI Gibson drove slightly faster than he should
have back to the police station, but he was anxious
to see the look on Gary's face when he told him
he was being arrested for theft of the
town's chocolate.

Chapter seventeen

The confession

Tuesday 24th

"The interview today is with Mr Smith, his solicitor

Mr Porter, DC Hamilton and myself, DI Gibson,"

the detective said.

Gary looked horrified.

"So, Gary, guess what we found at your home?"

"No comment."

"We have uncovered a secret room, and in that

room, we have found a very large amount of

chocolate. Do you have any explanation for this?"

"No comment."

"We could go on like this for hours and hours. I ask you a simple question and all you reply is 'no comment'." DI Gibson slammed his hand on the table in anger.

"Sorry," Gary mumbled.

"Are you going to start explaining to me why you have boxes and boxes of chocolate in your house, hidden behind a false wall, and also a pipe of chocolate leading from the factory, to a huge cooking pot."

Mr Smith started to cry. "I was only doing it for their own good."

"Whose own good, Gary?" DI Gibson asked.

"The children. I care about them so much and every day all they want to eat is chocolate."

"So, you are telling me that you stole all the chocolate for that reason?"

"Not all of it. There are still a few places left to steal from." Gary sniffed.

"Not anymore, it's over now, Gary."

"There was nothing else I could do."

"You went to all this trouble to steal every bar of chocolate in the town to stop the children eating it?" DI Gibson was confused.

"Yes, I did."

"Well, thank you for the confession, Gary, although I am still confused. Why?"

"Every day, I see those children getting larger and larger and their teeth getting dirtier and dirtier, all because they eat chocolate. I thought if I stole all the chocolate, then the children wouldn't be able to eat any more."

"That is almost unbelievable. Surely you must have realised that you would be caught eventually?"

"Yes, but it was worth it, even if it was only for a short time." Gary put his head in his hands and cried uncontrollably.

Chapter eighteen

The television film crew

Wednesday 25th

None of the teachers asked any of the children to do any work. Everyone just sat and talked about Mr Smith and his arrest. It didn't take long for the news to report that Mr Smith was the chocolate thief. The local news reported on the story all of yesterday evening. There was even an extended news programme reporting on the events of the day.

"The police have confirmed today that a thirty-seven-year-old man, Gary Smith, the headteacher from the local Marshmallow Junior School, has been arrested for the recent spate

of chocolate thefts in the town."

"To think he blamed me for all of these thefts," Billy announced to his classmates.

"He was obviously trying to cover his tracks," a classmate replied.

"It was a pretty rash thing to do, to stop us eating all the chocolate." Billy remarked.

After lunch, a television film crew arrived. They were looking for students of the school who were willing to go on camera and speak about the chocolate thief. They were making a documentary. Any children that were interested were asked to go to the sports hall, where the television crew would be filming.

When Billy arrived, almost every student from the school was waiting in the hall.

A camera and a microphone were thrown in front of Billy's face.

"So how do you feel, lad?" the reporter asked.

"Billy, my name is Billy."

"Billy, how do you feel?"

"I am relieved the thief has been caught," Billy

explained.

"Why is that, Billy?"

"Mr Smith was constantly accusing me of being the thief. When all along it was him."

"That is awful to hear. Why did Mr Smith accuse you?"

"Because I love chocolate so much."

"Most of the children do, Billy. Isn't that why Mr Smith did it? Because he wanted all the children to stop eating chocolate." The reporter smiled.

"It makes sense, but he didn't have to become a chocolate thief."

"Very true, but he obviously thought he was helping," the reporter replied.

"What will happen to Mr Smith now?" Billy asked.

"I am sure he will spend a long time in prison for his crime."

"Maybe I could send him a parcel of chocolate whilst he is in prison. Hopefully, that will cheer him up." Billy smiled.

Acknowledgements

I would like to thank many people who have helped me to get my book onto the shelves.

Firstly, my son. We have had many discussions regarding this story and he has given me many ideas on how to make the story even more fun.

A huge thanks to the photographer, Karen Kodish, who took the promotional photos for me.

Jamie Doodle, who has drawn some wonderful illustrations; these illustrations have really brought my book to life.

I would like to thank my editor, Hannah McCall, from Black Cat Editorial Services, for supplying great editorial support.

I also would like to thank my graphic designer, Elliot Willis at Willis Design Associates, for setting the book out, with the illustrations and creating the cover.

I wish to thank my friends and family who have given me the support I have needed whilst working on The Chocolate Thief.

Last, but by no means the least, I wish to thank you all for reading my book.

If you wish to contact me, my details are:

Kathkirklandauthor@gmail.com
www.kathkirklandauthor.co.uk

I am always happy to receive messages from my readers.
If you have enjoyed this book, please leave a review on Amazon (if you are under thirteen, please ask an adult to do this for you).

Kath Kirkland

Printed in Great Britain
by Amazon

56278452R00072